THE

<< LINE-STORY>>

The Nation's Newest Pastime

Godfrey H. Holmes

The Line-Story

First published : October 2009 by

NETHERMOOR BOOKS
<< Nethermoor >>
32 Miriam Avenue,
Somersall,
Chesterfield
Derbyshire
S40 3NF

Telephone 01246-566069

Any questions about Line-Storytelling :
godfrey.holmes@btinternet.com

A catalogue record for this book is available from the British Library

ISBN : 978-0-9536016-2-2

WHAT IS A LINE-STORY ?

A Line - Story is a complete

tale of between

eight and twelve words -

with either a beginning,

a middle and an end ;

OR a natural progression

from situation to resolution.

THE LINE-STORY GETS ITS NAME FROM TYPEWRITER AND COMPUTER TYPEFACES WHICH ALLOWED AN AVERAGE OF TWELVE WORDS PLUS PER LINE

CONTENTS

GENERAL INTRODUCTION

Courses for fledgling writers often began with the wickedly simple question :

" What is the shortest story ever written ? "

Answer :

" I'm expecting."
" Oh no ! Whose is it ? I'll kill him! "

Ten words. Then the tutor wants stories altogether more substantial : still home-made - but a thousand words in length, written with depth, texture and varying perspective.

But I, for one, long to linger where we have begun. Because - as for many other people - over the years, my reading habits have changed.

I used to become absorbed in an entire novel. Then half the novel....skipping to the ending after 130 pages or so : to see how tension is resolved ; seeing how all the characters make out.

Later : I could manage only the first 70 or 80 pages, before losing interest....justifying my distractedness in these terms:

" Well : it's all made up, anyway" ;
" Do I *really care* about these people ? "

There followed twenty years of preferring Non-fiction : transport and architecture ,biography and autobiography, history and geography, politics and sociology .

Then, quite unexpectedly, I came across a section in our Central Library (rather patronizingly) called :
BEDTIME READING.

Soon I became immersed in Scottish and Canadian Short Stories, women's and travellers' Short Stories, humorous and ghostly Short Stories ; also the Short Stories of Kipling and Saki, Thomas Hardy, Somerset Maugham.

Short Stories fitted the modern age - the shorter, the better.

No practitioner of the 3 to 8-page Short Story struck me as gifted to the same extent as Guy de Maupassant. Most of his stories (all originally written in the French Language) were, and are, available in English translation too.

Even so, *Non-fiction* still tugged me with the stronger rope. Isn't it strange ? - I used to ask myself, and still do - that half of *all writing ever crafted* is called by the negative !

It is as if all vegetables were called " NON-fruit " and all day-wear : " NON-pyjama. "

Thus I scaled down to the one- page Short Story, then the shorter Short Story ; finally : the Mini-Saga…. stuff of Weekend-Supplement competitions : fifty words (crucially, excluding the title that can tell half the story !) with a beginning, a middle and an end.

Then, still not satisfied, I re-invented THE LINE-STORY : that soundbite of a Short Story, maximum twelve words, occupying a single line of type or computer-print.

As my model for any Mini-Story I take a passage from history :
from the Second Book of Samuel in the Old Testament :
<< How are the mighty fallen ! >> …..five words.

These five words encapsulate arrival (ie. movement), acute observation, past *and* future action.

This is a reporter on the battlefield - in the danger zone - preparing his despatch for the next news bulletin.

Here he sums up a dreadful scene : renowned and armoured fighters, probably also the first on the scene, cruelly mown down like blades of grass.

This reporter urgently wants to tell others - us - what he has seen with his own eyes. All in five words !

It is *not* true that ALL single sentences can become Line-Stories.

Millions of single sentences are completely inconsequential I am deeply moved by Dorothy Rowe's quote :

<< *To all the world a soldier he ; to me, all the world."* >> This keeps to twelve words but is, primarily, *an observation* rather than an approximate story.

So Line-Stories have to stand or fall by their deviation from other literary forms :-

* Quotations. Many quotations - unlike Samuel's - tell no story.

* Aphorisms or Truisms ;

* Commands and Instructions. These might be poetical - but do not add up to complete narrative ;

* First Lines of Poems . Most miss the target, but Stevie Smith's : " Not Waving - but Drowning, " is superb ;

* Advertizing slogans : for example -
" Murray Mints, Murray Mints : the Too-Good-To-Hurry Mints." Ten words indeed, but not ones which tell a storyeir story so immediately, and memorably, as :
" When the dirt says HOT, and the label says NOT : use...;"

* Political sound-bites like : " Back to Basics." With " Back to Basics, " John Major was brilliantly evoking a time when Britain was quiet and orderly, imperious and imperial. But the majority of political sound-bites do not show electors ways to progress from starting-point to finishing-line ;

* Haiku. Line-Stories face their fiercest competition from Haiku : the Japanese verse- form consisting of 17 syllables in three lines of five, seven and five syllables respectively. Haiku poems express a single idea, image or feeling , as in Kirkup's :

<< In the amber dusk
Each island dreams its own night.
The sea swarms with gold. >>

Despite the impenetrability of Japanese culture , some British schools develop brilliant lessons around Haiku. I have seen wonderful Haiku on the display-boards of quite deprived inner-city Primaries ;

* Tanka : a related Japanese form of 31 syllables ;

* Proverbs. " Too many cooks spoil the broth." Yes, this is a kind of story. Many Proverbs are observational tales.

* Song titles.
These too are inventive : " U Don't have to call, " or " The Only Living Boy in New Cross, "- but they still fail the corridor test for Line Stories.

****

Let us therefore set a challenge, in schools, in residential establishments, churches, clubs, societies, and libraries, to produce passionate and purposeful Line-Stories, twelve, or fewer, words in length.

And let newspapers, magazines, and colour supplements also throw down the gauntlet : the creation, or the completion, of the perfect Line-Story.

To start everyone off here are three of my own :

<< Boosting library loans, bank-notes are randomly hidden.
But greedy punters , anarchically, stampede. >>

<< First day : new car. Flash floods rise relentlessly.
Second day : old car. >>

<< Unwary volunteers spilling secrets. Studio audiences guffawing. Discerning viewers switching channel. >>

****

SUMMARY OF THE COUSINS

OF THE LINE-STORY

* A STORY-LINE IS A LINE OR PARAGRAPH DESCRIBING HOW A STORY WILL PROGRESS (SIMILAR TO A PLOT)

---

* AN ANECDOTE IS A SHORT STORY OR REMINISCENCE : USUALLY A PECULIAR OR AMUSING HAPPENING (perhaps 200-300 words long)

---

* APHORISMS or PROVERBS ARE WISE SAYINGS -of up to 20 words - like :
  " a stitch in time saves nine " – or
  " too many cooks spoil the broth "

---

* A MORAL IS LIKE A PROVERB : THE UNDERLYING MESSAGE OF A STORY OR AN ANECDODE –
  for instance :
  " only pigs are found with their snouts in the trough."

---

* A MINI-SAGA IS A SHORT STORY OF MAXIMUM 50 or 60 WORDS - WITH A BEGINNING, A MIDDLE and AN END.

---

* A SHORT STORY IS A STORY OR A NOVELLA OF 500 to 5000 WORDS

---

* A SHORT, SHORT-STORY IS ANOTHER NAME FOR A MINI-SAGA

---

* HAIKU IS A JAPANESE VERSE OF EXACTLY 17 SYLLABLES : first line = 5 syllables second-line = 7 syllables, third line = 5 syllables

---

* TANKA IS A RELATED JAPANESE FORM OF 31 SYLLABLES

---

* A COMMAND IS A SINGLE LINE OR TWO LINES OF INSTRUCTION :
for instance : " Door only to be used in Emergencies "!

---

* A FIRST-LINE IS THE (usually memorable) FIRST LINE OF A POEM OR SONG like :
" And did those feet, in ancient times.....? " (Blake)

---

* A TEXT IS A SENTENCE -usually Biblical - UNDERLYING A SPEECH or a SERMON :
for instance : " Never flag in zeal ; be aglow
with the Spirit."

---

* A QUOTATION IS A (USUALLY FAMOUS) ENTRY OF UP TO 50 WORDS - WORTH REMEMBERING YEARS LATER - like :
" A week is a long time in Politics " (Harold Wilson)

---

* A TWITTER IS AN 140-CHARACTER, MAXIMUM, TEXT-BASED POSTING ON AN AUTHOR'S SITE

---

* A SIX-WORD MEMOIR IS A MINI-BIOGRAPHY POPULARIZED BY *SMITH MAGAZINE* (plus later variants incl. SIX-WORD LOVE STORY)

>> readers will know of *many other* one-line formats

THE GREATEST MINI-STORY EVER TOLD :

VENI , VIDI, VICI

" I CAME,

I SAW,

I CONQUERED "

written in a letter by
Julius Caesar (100 - 44 B.C.)
announcing victory in the last
battle of the Pontic campaign.

****

POSSIBLE USES FOR THE LINE STORY :

** to construct on a long car-journey

** to construct in train or plane

** to construct when waiting in a long queue

** to construct in the middle of the night….
as a remedy for sleeplessness

** to borrow or to construct as part of a collection

** to add to a greetings-card, or envelope

** to fill a space in a school- or a parish-magazine

** in competition within an English lesson

** in competition against brother, sister, or parent

** inter-school, or national-magazine competition

** first - or last - words supplied , with a challenge to find the 6 or 7 words in between

****

BREAKING DOWN THE LINE-STORY :

2 words / 2 words / 2 words

3 words / 3 words / 3 words / 3 words

4 words / 4 words / 4 words

6 words / 6 words

12 (or fewer than 12) **words.... all at once -**

OR one of these sequences :

3/6/3, 2/8/2

2/6/2, 3/2/2/2/3

3 - 4 - 3, 5 - 2 - 5, 2 - 3 - 3 - 2, 2 - 4 - 4 - 2,

2 - 3 - 4 , 3 - 4 - 5, 4 - 3 - 4, 2 - 2- 2 - 2 - 2 - 2

or any sequence that adds up to 8, 9, 10, 11 or 12 words.

****

FILLING IN THE LINE – STORY :

Some Line-Stories deliberately come to us *incomplete.*

Here are a few possible ways of creating missing gaps (gaps are normally best left in the standard *12-line* Story) :

>> **1st. word only given**

>> **1st. two words given**

>> **Introduction, only, given**

>> **Middle word - or words - given**

>> **Last word only given**

>> **Last two words given**

>> **Ending , only, given**

>> **Every alternate word given.**

The beauty of the *incomplete* Line-Story is the possibility - and the freedom - to complete the 12 words in any way that makes sense. Uniquely. With no chance someone else will get there first.

This assignment is similar to competitions seen on the outside of groceries (less commonly, these days) :

" Complete this slogan in under 20 words….."

Some children's puzzle-books are also written with exercises concentrating on the missing word(s). However, in puzzle books (books now aimed at grown-ups too), a random list of missing words, *not infrequently, a list longer than the number of blank spaces available*, is also supplied.

Opinions vary as to whether a hyphenated word : eg. deck-hand, criss-cross, meeting-point….. is one word or two.

For the purpose of the Line-Story, it makes sense to count linked words as one word…with the exception of

" Pig-in-the-middle " !

***

Most Line-Stories lack a *TITLE*. Yet in certain Mini-Saga competitions, titles are allowed.

The title can easily compensate for the restricted number of words in the Line-Story / Mini Saga itself.
So, here, there is an opening for writing a Line-Story after being given its title OR giving *the best* title to a Line-Story that has been created already by someone else.

In the absence of title - or title challenge - another possibility presents itself : the *THEME*.

In this book, most Line-Stories have a theme : eg. *BOREDOM* or *ASKING A QUESTION* headlined at the beginning of a particular section.

But there is no reason why an *ANGLE* or a *CLUE* cannot be set for forthcoming Line-Stories.

For instance, for Line-Stories surrounding Building, the angle could be : cost, materials, or space - whilst the clue could be aborted house removal, unsightly bird droppings - or a terminated purchase.

****

A newcomer to Line-Stories possibly believes there are only four or five ways 12 words can be arranged.

That is too pessimistic. There are *thousands* of potential completions, especially when no help or theme, no clue or angle, is supplied. Thus it is very unlikely two people in separate rooms could ever come up with an identical story.

****

PRODUCING A LINE – STORY

AGAINST THE CLOCK

A good Line-Story probably takes between 5 and 20 minutes to write.

Producing original Line-Stories is a very tiring business. Much simpler is *writing to a formula* such as in my section on *WARNINGS.*

If a family or a pub, a radio programme or a school classroom gives competitors a strict time-limit to come up with a Line-Story, then a period of between 1 and 4 minutes might be appropriate.

There is still no absolute safeguard to prevent the appearance of a borrowed or trite or stale Line-Story.

But this can be countered by a strong dose of *surprise* in the assignment : a Line-Story set in Oxford or London, concerning Bears or Donkeys, on a Sunday or Monday.

Other ways of approaching a time limit is to set 6 or 8 Line Stories at the same time, to say : " Whoever finishes first………" - or to ask for all Line-Stories to arrive at a certain address within seven or ten days.

Time limits are not *automatically* a good idea - or the right approach.

It is certainly possible to spend *too long* producing a Story - and the Story isn't always better for all the effort. If one subject or one approach is not working, better to give up - or to alter the assignment.

Thirty Stories per day is about the maximum for anybody really concentrating.

****

TRAGEDY IN THE LINE- STORY

The importance of Tragedy in the Line-Story is the same as Tragedy underlying most News, Theatre, Everyday Life - Comedy indeed !

Tragedy is never far removed from joy.

Joy, happiness, beneficial outcome : logically, these should feature in all human drama - and its reportage - as much as Tragedy. But that is rarely the case.

Some daily and Sunday newspapers have special 50-word boxes for tragedies that have happened in the past 24 hours : tragedies not significant enough to merit a full-page or a double spread, but snippets of news worth noting for posterity. How often these news-bites make arouse curiosity!

In actual fact , these short " fillers " are not significantly different from Mini-Sagas, except for the addition of *identifiable* names and places and consequences.

Tragic Line-Stories are also easier to write than happy ones. The demise, destruction or denouement come quickly and more forcibly than when *success* needs relaying.

****

HANDY TIPS FOR CONSTRUCTING TRAGIC LINE-STORIES

---

* **Draw some tragedies from what you have experienced ;**

* **Draw other tragedies from the newspapers ;**

* **Draw even more tragedies from what you have heard has happened to other people ;**

* **Complete your sources from radio and TV ;**

* **Describe a tragedy actually unfolding ;**

* ***Or* describe a tragedy averted at the last minute;**

* **Understate the tragedy, rather than Overstating it ;**

* **Keep explicit descriptions like :
" As the knife went in, it was twisted….."
to an absolute minimum ;**

* **Leave part of the tragedy to the imagination ;**

* **and… Use some very unusual words.**

SOME EXAMPLES OF TRAGIC LINE - STORIES

>> Collecting conkers, straying dangerously, Jim's head hit van.....just like a conker.

>> Geologist Adam achieved his ambition. One crater - much greater - reclaimed its own.

>> HILTON's notice : " DO NOT DISTURB " lingered six days. Diabetic Annette lingered four.

>> Single boulder, perchance, kills one tourist. Wonderful " Marine Drive " bars *all* tourists.

>> After earthquake rattles Cathedral, engineers inspecting damage buried beneath priceless murals....tumbling.

>> Whilst researching ancient lead-mines, dentist discovers one : uncapped - too late.

>> Distraught woman leaps from tower block : flattening a pedestrian, but saving herself.

>>   Swimmers swim contentedly ;
Lifeguards chat merrily ;
Nobody notices Noreen underwater -
gasping….sinking.

>> The intrepid war photographer films his own demise.
Advancing warriors stay   anonymous.

>> Gripping, edging, mounting, surveying.
Flinging, stretching, diving, straightening,
Bracing, entering, striking…..tombstoning.

>>Lucy's parent trusted her imagined kidnapper.
Lucy's kidnapper, panicking,   distrusted her parent.

>>All Christmas Day, suicide negotiators negotiated ;
at darkfall, the leaper leapt, unrestrained.

>> As ball bowled at wicket,
the lorry sheds its spare wheel : fatally.

>> Quaintly, perennially, Gozoan peasants shoot pheasants.
Vainly, they warn tourists pathfinding thereabouts.

>> Gleeful soldiers tilt the dreaded waterboard –

oblivious to terrified suspect spluttering….choking.

>> How neatly he decapitated his wife :
she holding, unsteadily, ladder to hedge.

>> Mazy's kitchen flooded - like a lake - each October :
ruining each January's renovation.

>> Intentionally careering off the motorway,
Jim rebounded , unharmed, to crush the innocents.

>> Only on his roof to save aerial bills,
concrete walkways finished Timothy.

>> Those gallant divers never resurfaced.
That galleon's treasure remained undisturbed.

>> *He* registering each distant spire, tower or turret,
She, jogging, remained unseen.

>> Why did Tom only book a single
The day the rollercoaster malfunctioned ?

****

TRAGIC LINE-STORIES WITH GAPS

One sunny
Spring____

Suddenly
awakened____

Losing
money____

____

>>____against the odds.

>>____leading to decline.

>>____to Carol's pleasure.

>>__________________________rape__________________

____

>>_________________________murder__________________

____

>>_________________________offence__________________

____

the
student____

the
teacher____

the
doctor____

CREATING BRAND NEW TRAGIC LINE - STORIES :

TELEVISION LINE - STORIES

Some Examples :

>> Her audience laughed until they cried.
Her contestant cried until she fled.

>> Ambitiously broadcasting seventy-six channels ;
unadventurously watching five.

>> So long recalling seeing actress act before ;
so little *enjoying* her acting.

>> The camera-shot changes in *Casualty* ; calamity follows.

>> They boo, hiss, shout down the judge.
Only *she* takes it seriously.

>> Tired of repeats, Albert kicks telly out the window -
completely flattening passer-by.

>> After warm-up, the audience is excitable.
No contestant shines that night.

>> Supermarket's trolley-dash proved frenetic.
How he loved his canned lager !

>> The audience was supposed to sing *spontaneously*
... until cameras, erringly, featured conductor.

>> How stern - distant - the correspondent appeared -
except when his colleague lay dying.

>> Apologies. Apologies. The newscaster has gremlins.
No apologies : the newscaster has chutzpah.

>> They slandered the black footballer mercilessly.
That afternoon, sound filters overcame everything.

>> Wendy wedded to her soaps had
bathroom, bedroom, kitchen, *lounge*
broadcasting facilities !

****

TELEVISION LINE - STORIES WITH GAPS

On __________at 1am

____

Switching
over____

Brenda could not
watch____

>>____leaving
him sickened.

____exhausting
her patience

>>____deflating
the star.

>>__________________________Panorama_________________

____

The News____

>>____________________Coronation Street_________

____

>>____the presenter_____________________________

____

>>______________the producer____________________

____

>>_______the stand-in__________________________

____

CREATING BRAND NEW TELEVISION LINE STORIES :

RADIO LINE - STORIES

Some Examples :

>> Driving, Caroline answered the radio back.
Stalled, the laughing machine chortled irrepressibly.

>> Throughout love-making, the radio symphony orchestra played.
Crescendo. Diminuendo. Then silence.

>> The hairdresser never switched her wireless off.
Fed up, her customers defected.

>> Radio news accompanied family meals : 8, 1, 6.
Disaster. Rape. Pillage. Divorce.

>> At 81, the actor still played schoolboy.
At 82, schoolboys attended funeral.

>> Betimes, Rosalind's fine voice croaked breaking news.
Evermore, dry throats tormented her.

>> Alf left radio on whilst at pub.
Burglar sat down to listen.

>> "   Radio has the best pictures "   :
so dedicated, unsociable,   ramblers - with I-pods -
discovered.

>> The newborn baby loved that box.
She chuckled. She gurgled. She   " understood."

>> Radio relieved the apprentices' boredom mending cars :
" Analysis ",   " Face the Facts ",   " Moneybox ".

>> " Afternoon Play " got so weird,
even its producer couldn't think straight.

>> "   Daily Service " sounded so holy,
even *Continuity* knelt down reverently.

>> " In Town Today " proved so interesting,
the Maddoxes stayed put !

****

RADIO LINE - STORIES WITH GAPS

Radio Nottingham
decided____

One politician
sounded____

Hospital Radio
startled____

>>____until its end.

>>______________________________________floods of tears.

>>_____________________________________ libel settled.

>>________________________" Analysis "__________

____

" The Archers"____________________________________

____

" Any Questions ? "________________________________

____

>>_________the Editor____________________________

>>______the Interviewee ________________________

____

>>______the Sound Engineer________________

____

****

CREATING BRAND NEW RADIO LINE-STORIES

LINE-STORIES OF DANCE

Some examples :

>> Nobody doubted this couple's ice-skating skills - except each other.
Remorselessly, they bickered.

>> Twisting thrice, he won gold.
Tumbling thrice, he left the tournament.

>> At village Tea Dance , Alec gracefully, gratefully, chose Alice….
until halitosis' onset.

>> Spurned on the sidelines overmuch,
Mavis exacted revenge crisscrossing the dance floor.

>> Earl's break-dancing was so skilled,
everyone - staying seated - watched , entranced.

>> The barn dance was boisterous, raucous.
Co-opted, press-ganged, cajoled : *everyone* responded.

>> Recollecting pre-War dance cards , Sylvester (to astonishment) used them on a cruise.

>> Suspecting immorality at gigs, one (youthful) parent went along.
How daughter blushed !

>> Each disco ended smashing plaster plates on skulls.
One plate was china !

>> Dance rules were tuxedo - but one participant, ex-participant, chose smart striped blazer.

>> Animosity developed on *Strictly Come Dancing* when Amateur performed better than Professional.

>> Alice, 3, danced wonderfully to records.....
unintentionally giving granddad a sinister thrill.

****

DANCE LINE-STORIES WITH GAPS

>>________________________fell______________________

>>Late evening____________________________________

>>___________I yearned___________________________

>>On STRICTLY,_______________________________

____

>________________ the ice______________________

****

CREATE YOUR OWN DANCE LINE-STORY :

" Don't worry : they always chat throughout performances."
" Tonight they don't ! "

Swiftly the headmistress yanked camera out of Mum's hand during their Nativity.

" Poor little mite : forgot his lines.... "
Poor big audience. They deserved better.

The Company worked " miracles " on bad scripts.
Unconvinced critics closed their theatre.

An ingenious trap-door elevated scenery.
It also swallowed actors.

BOO ! HISS ! RUBBISH ! TRASH !
The audience rioted.
Were they orchestrated ?
No.

Their producer soothes hurt egos by giving *everybody* a role next time.

The theatre humiliated its greedy seat-swappers :
six paid " late-comers."

GOLDILOCKS was so popular it lasted fourteen months : perpetual pantomime.

" The Royal " never did sort out its acoustics.
Sound engineers slept soundly.

21st Century HAMLET. 21st. Century prices.

Upbeat, downbeat, heartfelt, frivolous :
whatever transpired, the sunken orchestra repeated its " range."

****

CREATE YOUR OWN THEATRICAL LINE-STORY:

FILM LINE-STORIES

Hollywood, Bollywood, Spaghetti Western, Czech Epic :
home-grown Cinema never sounded so captivating.

<< *Princess of Glamour* >> : interview her only 15 minutes.
" Next ! " " Next ! " " Where's next ? "

Threadbare red carpets for prize ceremonies :
gold, silver, prizes for threadbare performances.

Two died doing stunts for this blockbuster .
Complimentary tickets for two widows.

" Shush ! " " *Shush !* " " Quiet ! "
As kiddies spilled out, the usherette's nervous collapse deepened.

" This is the film you can take your parents to." Clean. Spotless.

" Long Mackintosh's " pre-recorded films all had wholesome covers :
you couldn't find exception.

Alley trader supreme : his custom was filming films.
And fakes attracted custom.

No childhood tale survived the celluloid.
So scenes horrific horrified loyal readers.

As credits rolled, the audience fled.
Except one teenager. Except one Director.

Sing travelling to " *Sound of Music.* " Sing throughout.
Sing going home.

" Audiences are specifically asked not to imitate this scene. "
Or else.

Bellfield's cinema was miraculously rescued by " white knight."
Arsonists arrived. Darkest night

****

CREATE YOUR OWN FILM LINE-STORY

MODERN-TECHNOLOGY LINE-STORIES

Darren was a techno-pioneer - always *first* acquiring technology :
retarded - *last* - conversing.

He lived by the Internet, died : aided by the Internet. Beyond censor.

In Cyberspace, Bill and Ben prosper.
Outdoors : Bill and Ben flounder.

31 Pupils. 31 confiscated mobiles. 31 angry complaints. One dismissal.

40 tonnes. 40 texts. 40 phone-calls. 40 die, crushed, in burning coach.

More telephoning one day than one (recent) year : life lived vicariously. Precariously.

This screen is *bigger, clearer, wider* : three tellies dumped, three dustmen entertained.

Computers water flowers, draw curtains, extinguish lights.....and bring down holiday aeroplanes.

Typewriter ribbon : £ 2 - delight.   Inkjet : £ 22 - misery.

Cynthia could not sleep lest she miss worldwide prices :
a priceless loss.

The microchip revolutionized the West - bringing it down.
The chips *are* down.

****

CREATE YOUR OWN MODERN-TECHNOLOGY LINE-STORY

WARNING LINE- STORIES

<< NOTICE : Magnets are fitted to this lavatory seat. >>
(amputees beware !)

<< WARNING ! Rocks falling ! >>
(biggest danger : rocks dropped already)

<< DANGER : AVALANCHES ! >>
(greater danger : starting one off)

<< BEWARE ! Electricity kills ! >>
(but I thought that windswept cable
presented no hazard)

<< DANGER ! Unsafe masonry >>
(however, I'm a demolition
contractor....Greater danger !)

<< MIND THE GAP ! >>
(gangplank requested....but gangplank *itself*
needs anchor)

<< BEWARE : WORKMEN AT WORK ! >>
(but are you aware it's their tea-break ?)

<< HAZARD ! DEEP WATER ! >>
(how deep ? very deep .....see for yourself !)

<< ATTENTION ! THIN ICE ! >>
(it held Harry yesterday when he lost his ball !)

<< DANGER ! ALCOHOL RUINS LIVES ! >>
(well it certainly hasn't ruined Gertie's !)

****

CREATE YOUR OWN WARNING LINE-STORY :

LINE-STORIES ABOUT CHILDREN

3 EXAMPLES

1) " Children should be seen and not heard " upstairs, 24/7, on a laptop.

2) Eventually deciding to play hopscotch, two boys contested alleged foot-faults bitterly.

3) Teachers said the phase would pass - but Amy never relinquished Enid Blyton.

GAPS

The game of
marbles______________________________________

The matinee
film____

Immediately after
school___________________________________

>>____fits
of laughter.

Page 52

>>____on the pavement.

>>____________________________________damaging sofa springs.

>>_____________________playing nurses_________

____

>>_____________________wounded finger________

____

>>_____________________another baby___________

____

>>______dining room _________________

____

>>________beach_______________________________

____

>_______ruler_________________________________

CREATING BRAND NEW LINE-STORIES AROUND CHILDREN

(Remembering :
your own childhood -
OR your own children, and their escapades
OR children in general : adults who haven't lived so long)

AMUSING LINE-STORIES

3 EXAMPLES :

1) Mum - soaked through to the skin -
only wanted 8 minutes' jet-wash.

2) His car swaying gently atop the stone wall,
Greg telephoned the Insurance.

3) Hearing the crowd's mirth,
only PooPoo the Clown resented the upturned trifle.

GAPS :

One Monday
morning____

Hidden in the
cupboard_______________________________________

The choir
stopped____

____
>>_____________________________________in the loft.

>>____

stark naked.

>>_______________________________________

needing re-painting.

>>____________________balloons__________________

____

>>____________________red wine_______________

____

>>____________________caravan__________________

____

>>_______the burglar____________________________

____

>>____

excitement.

>>______extraordinary hat______________________

CREATING BRAND NEW LINE-STORIES THAT ARE AMUSING

(Remembering
amusing incidents in your own life
OR amusing happenings in the newspaper -
OR funny objects) :

LINE - STORIES WITH A HAPPY ENDING

3 EXAMPLES :

1) After 64 moves in 32 years, the gypsies -anonymously- bought a field.

2) For 12 days this holidaying family bickered.
They enjoyed Day 13 enormously.

3) Lacerated overseas, Juliette's body remained undiscovered.
Found, reassuringly, it reached Scarborough's graveyard.

GAPS :

Tuesday
started____

A poor
lecture____

____

A single postcard____

>>____leading to closure.

>>____without despairing.

>>____

at last.

>>__________________________argument__________________

____

>>_________________________wrong table_______________

____

>>___________________________swimming_______________

>>_________ the donkey______________________________

____

>>__________tablets_____________________________________

>>______________________________some comfort________

CREATING BRAND NEW - LINE STORIES ENDING HAPPILY

(*Remembering*
Improbably good outcomes in your own life
OR a progression from dissent to agreement
OR a transformation from despair to hope)

TWIST-IN-THE-TAIL LINE STORIES

3 EXAMPLES :

1) Miraculously found at foot of cliffs !
Pensioner protests : " I don't want rescuing ! "

2) Jilted at the altar,
one guest knew this would happen : the bride.

3) 888888 won her (heaven-sent) £ 1000 on scratch card. Silver smithereens obscured 888388.

GAPS :

After the
celebration____

Opening the
envelope_______________________________________

One
Sunday____

>>____

_______________________in court.

>>____

under the bed.

>>____

from the past.

>>________________________sausages________________

____

>>________________________mackintoshes____________

____

>>_______________________the tree________________

____

>>_______the adverrtisement_______________________

____

>>______badges___________________________________

____

>>______a bishop_________________________________

CREATING BRAND NEW TWIST-IN-THE-TAIL LINE- STORIES

(Remembering

** that 12 words is not long for a complex ending ;*

** that other Line Stories also have unexpected endings ;*

**that there is some difference between coincidence and surprise.*)

LINE-STORIES WITH ANIMALS

3 EXAMPLES :

1) Twelve piglets needed round-the-clock surveillance.
The sow lay on one.

2) Gabriella's horse butted and tormented ramblers for fun.
Gabriella, unfazed, laughed heartily.

3) " Bonzo " that bit the postman was not destroyed.
He was a twin.

GAPS :

The rampaging
bull____

Out of their
hutch____

Tethered
goats____

>>____

over the fence.

>>____to the slaughter.

____forever loved.

>>____________________stable__________________________

____

>>_______________________dying grass_________________

____

>>_______________________one flock___________________

____

>>________ domesticated cat___________________________

____

>>________pedigree pup______________________________

____

>>______elephant______________________________________

____

CREATING BRAND NEW LINE-STORIES WITH ANIMALS

(Remembering :

* *animals are not human ;*
  * *Your own experiences with pets :*
    * *AND- the whole range of animals in the wild. Perhaps include fishes.)*

L I N E-S T O R I E S A R O U N D R E L I G I O N

3 EXAMPLES :

1) Losing his faith, the vicar still managed two decades' faithful service.

2) The preacher heard so many AMENs , he began leaving gaps between exhortations.

3) Saving hefty entrance fees, Wendy visited cathedrals on Sunday mornings.

GAPS :

At exactly 6pm.________________________________

____

During a long prayer____

Outside the chapel____

>>____for Midnight Mass.

>>____in perpetuity.

>>______________________________________behind the mosque.

>>_______________________readings___________________

____

>>_____________________the faithful___________________

____

>>_______________________shaking hands_____________

____

>>_______hymnal____________________________________

>>_______the Imam________________________________

____

>>_______in Sunday School_______________________

____

CHRISTMAS LINE-STORIES

3 EXAMPLES :

1) In the bleak Midwinter, the Broadbents did not celebrate Christmas : " completely pointless."

2) Angels graced Angela's calendar, wall, towel, notepad. Angels graced Angela's life too.

3) Boxing Day snow prevented four parents-in-law meeting before January's factional Wedding.

GAPS :

For Christmas
Dinner____

Before the
sleigh____

The Christmas
Bazaar____

>>____day to

remember.

>>______________________________________damaged presents.

>>____

tree lights.

>>_________________________snowman______________

____

>>_________________________roast turkey___________

>>________________________carol singing___________

____

>>_____________holly__________________________

____

>>________too much work______________________

____

>>_________wrapping paper__________________

____

CREATING BRAND NEW LINE- STORIES FOR CHRISTMAS

(Remembering :
Happy or not-so-happy Christmases past -
OR the symbolism of Christmas
OR how other families and groupings adapt to this Festival)

LINE-STORIES FOR A BIRTHDAY

3 EXAMPLES :

1) Poor Sam cried, inconsolably, all birthday because nobody at all sent cards.

2) Her Birthday ended , ruinously, with the most horrible, appalling, bloodthirsty , fantasy film.

3) Two sisters - without reward - complained bitterly being born late December.

****

GAPS :

On birthday
morning,______________________________________

In one birthday
card____

Celebrating at
school______________________________________

>>____home

too late.

>>____the wrong make.

>>____

too excited.

>>___________________________surprise________________

____

>>__________________________the bumps______________

____

>>_________________________special cake_____________

____

>>_________Centenarian______________________________

____

>>_________new Pensioner__________________________

____

>>_______ special delivery_____________________

____

LINE-STORIES ABOUT SHOPPING

3 EXAMPLES :

1) In bachelor style, Guy did supermarket at 1am…. until, fatally, using ATM.

2) Gloria, personal shopper, secretly started shopping for herself, her client paying !

3) Six shelf-stackers got so bored, they stacked incorrectly but almost unnoticeably.

****

GAPS :

At
5-25____
____

On Checkout
21____

The
Manageress______________________________________

Page 74

>>____in the till.

>>____into the trolley.

>>____ was too much.

>>___________________________bags_________________ ____________

>>_________________________most sizes______________ ______________________

_______________________too few apples______________ _________________

>>_______stationery_________________________________

>>________cigarettes________________________________

>>____DIY.

CREATING BRAND NEW LINE-STORIES GOING SHOPPING

(*Remembering*

* *Shopping expeditions in the past*
  * *OR the atmosphere in a typical supermarket*
    * *OR what happens to purchases after being bought – or* <u>*to purchasers*</u>*, later on ?)*

LINE-STORIESABOUT FRIENDSHIP

3 EXAMPLES :

1) Many Mondays these disputatious lads healed Friday evening's drink-fuelled arguments.

2) Teenaged Christine could not keep in with Grace without (rather possessive) Mandy.

3) Both danced ; both hiked ; both gossiped ; both shopped *;* *both* guarded one secret.

****

GAPS :

Divided by
oceans_______________________________________

On their
mobiles_______________________________________

____

Forgetting
misunderstandings___________________________________

____

Page 77

>>____for the future.

>>____not returned.

>>___________________________________something unusual.

>>__________________the gatecrasher_____________

____

>>____________________a playground___________

____

>>____________________her diary_______________

____

>>________marriage____________________________

____

>>__________second kiss________________________

____

CREATING LINE - STORIES INCLUDING FRIENDSHIP

(Remembering

** some past friendships*

** OR the qualities of friendship*

** OR friendship across groupings normally set apart)*

LINE-STORIES ABOUT ENMITY

3 EXAMPLES :

1) Unreconciled, two brothers went half a Century not on speaking terms.

2) ORDERS didn't communicate with DESPATCH. Historically, they never had.

3) Rivalries only intensified after Edna's remarriage. Four sisters, two stepsisters, never adjusted.

****

GAPS :

After the funeral____

Redundancy notice in hand____

Two buddies____

____

>>____by

Christmas.

>>____without

trace.

>>____

despite mediation.

>>__________________after Church__________________

____

>>___________________________that e-mail____________

____

>>________________________train journey_____________

____

>>____

poison________

CREATE BRAND NEW LINE-STORIES INCLUDING ENMITY

(Remembering :
** the trickiest fallings out between people are UNDERSTATED and frequently unutterable ;*
** enmity can take on many disguises ;*
** AND our own memories of rift are often still all too fresh to revisit.)*

LINE- STORIES WHICH RHYME

3 EXAMPLES :

1) Husband each weekend in the garden ;
Her wish to leave *did harden.*

2) There was commotion in the street :
that's what happens when bikers meet.

3) Fourth time, our M.P. did lose .
Fifth time, one less to choose.

GAPS :

The boy____________________
The girl____________________

That day____________________
Next day____________________

Carol________________________
Darrel________________________

______________________the deep.
______________________good sleep.

Page 83

______________________bad news.
______________________your views.

______________________from us.
______________________off bus.

__________and_____________
__________and_____________

__________still_____________
__________till_______________

__________give_____________
__________take_____________

Ramblers_______________________
Gamblers_______________________

____________________________winning
____________________________sinning

****

CREATING NEW RHYMING LINE STORIES

Remembering :

not to make each rhyme too complicated ;
AND not to expect great poetry telling an
anecdote or a mini-story ;
AND not to use long words
In the beginning -
unless, very happily, an
ornament ryymes
with tournament!

LINE STORIES ABOUT WORK

3 EXAMPLES :

1) Peasants work the land - by hand - diligently, tirelessly, uncomplaining. Isn't that romantic ?

2) " Big Brother " conveyor-belt always fails mid-afternoon . Big bother.

3) She did 88 hours weekly : 44 employed , 44 housekeeping....For 88 weeks only !

****

GAPS :

On that shift____________________________________

____

Growing tired____

Told to go____

____

>>____
each Noon.

>>____causing
injury.

>>____felt
like play.

>>_____________________workshop_________________________

____

>>_______________________ the pit_____________________

____

>>____________________charityshop______________________

____

>>_______the nurse______________________________________

____

>>________foul play___________________________________

____

CREATING BRAND NEW LINE-STORIES SET AT WORK

(Remembering
your own days and experiences in paid
or unpaid or unexpected employment;
AND remembering how the workplace is
a great place for new friendships,
new ideas and new intrigues –
BUT also dreaded by many.)

LINE-STORIES AT THE OFFICE

3 EXAMPLES :

1) The office party was such a roaring success :
eight revellers never returned.

2) Why the office had 40000 unused envelopes,
only a kindhearted temp understood.

3) Office bullying intensified,
The sight of this Manager's car was threat sufficient.

****

GAPS :

Wilson
Brothers____

The office
clown____

One
Friday____

____

Page 89

>>____enjoy a jolly.

>>____stayed very late.

>>____in the cupboard.

>>______________________office romance____________

____

>>____________________far too busy_______________

____

>>______________________ called away_____________

____

>>________the photocopier_________________________

____

>>_________each telephone________________________

____

CREATING BRAND NEW LINE-STORIES ABOUT THE OFFICE

(*Remembering :*

* *the office is a rich forum for dissent and advance;*
* *the office is a meeting place for natural opposites and wicked rivals;*
* *AND offices tend to soak up all the energy devoted to them .)*

LINE-STORIES ABOUT FOOD

3 EXAMPLES :

1) " A third of all food is wasted. "
" In our home, it's half."

2) Mealtimes were to be dreaded .
Teenager Maria never wanted delicious meals.

3) The £2 chicken had a miserable life -
but customers - chickening out - never complained.

****

GAPS :

Her
groceries____

____

Each
Sunday____

____

Sharp knives________________________________

____

>>____under

the cupboard.

>>____in his basket.

____a baker's life.

>>_____________________the butchery______________

____

>>______________________bananas____________________

____

>>____________________rotting fish_________________

____

>>_______the delicatessen_________________________

LINE-STORIES ABOUT DRINK

3 EXAMPLES :

1) 200 parents offered padlocks for their fridges ;
2 parents using them.

2) A Thermos flask at today's football Derby.
Whoever would suspect anything untoward ?

3) Gwynneth's 21st. did not serve alcohol.
Her 77 gatecrashers " did not understand."

****

GAPS :

After the
party____

In the
graveyard_____________________________________

____

The pub______________________________________

____

>>____lie down.

>>____no nonsense.

____piles of bottles.

>>_______________________sherry_____________________

____

>>___________________fizzy___________________________

____

>>_______________________the lounge- bar____________

____

>>_______empty_____________________________________

>>________school dance____________________________

CREATING BRAND NEW LINE- STORIES CONTAINING FOOD OR DRINK

(*Remembering -*

* *to include drinks containing no alcohol, too ;*

* *AND situations where people do not get drunk –or over-eat;*

* *AND times where a simple act of eating and drinking has led to wider consequences)*

LINE-STORIES ABOUT NOSTALGIA

3 EXAMPLES :

1) Years spent sorting my untroubled past
could have sorted my troubled present.

2) Photograph albums fill every drawer, cupboard and box.
Does anybody open them ?

3) Victorian children so captured her imagination,
she dressed her own children Victorian.

****

GAPS :

Looking
back____

____

Collecting
antiques____

Revisiting
haunts____

____________disappointed.

Page 97

>>____

were reunited.

>>_______________________________cost too much.

>>_____________________old magazines______

____

>>_____________________good old days__________

____

>>____________________toys__________________

____

>>________love letters_____________________

____

>>________notebook___________________________

____

>>________kept diaries______________________

____

CREATING BRAND NEW NOSTALGIC LINE-STORIES

(Remembering -
** love of the past can take on many guises ;*
** everybody has a yearning to rediscover*
some part of childhood or the past :
in particular - and where they played.
**Matter-of-fact people still know*
others who are more
sentimental than them)

LINE-STORIES ABOUT FASHION

3 EXAMPLES :

1) She : a dedicated follower of fashion ;
He : a dedicated follower of passion.

2) Alan's labels all faced outwards .
Jamie was unfazed.
All his faced *inwards.*

3) So trendy was Mum's outfit for Parents' Evening,
Anna , eclipsed, felt ashamed.

****

GAPS :

That
handbag____

____

At the
Wedding____

____

Keeping up______________________________________

____

>>______________________________________threw it away.

>>____to OXFAM.

>>____in Lost Property.

>>____________________gloves_____________________

____

>>_____________________his overcoat_____________

____

>>_______________________price____________________

>>________boutique________________________________

____

>>________handing down___________________________

____

CREATING BRAND NEW LINE STORIES ABOUT FASHION

(*Remembering -*
** to include fashions outside of the wardrobe....*
** AND fashions which soon prove very unfashionable- or frumpy, by choice ;*
** getting into the mind of the fashion pioneer-or the fashion editor.)*

LINE - STORIES WITH MYSTERY

3 EXAMPLES :

1) A neat pile of clothes on the sand dune ;
no sight of the bankrupt.

2) Civil servants spent weeks, efficiently, tracking the whistleblower who leaked their inefficiencies.

3) The hotel's Murder Mystery was so fiendishly complex, no guest guessed whodunit.

****

GAPS :

Experienced
detectives______________________________________

The missing
clue____

Every
policeman_______________________________________

>>____in
that cabinet.

Page 103

>>____pointing fingers.

>>____Left Luggage.

>>___________________ _____fingerprints________________

____

>>___________________________gruesome death__________

____

>>_________________________the delivery___________

____

>>_________spy_______________________________________

____

>>__________the map__________________________________

>>__________family conference_______________________

____

CREATING BRAND NEW MYSTERIOUS LINE STORIES

(*Remembering :*

* *the best mysteries are never solved ;*
* *it's worth using real-life mysteries from the newspaper or a local TV news bulletin;*
* *Don't try to make these short mysteries too complex.*)

LINE STORIES SET IN HISTORY

3 EXAMPLES :

1) " Cakes burnt again ! " rasped Alfred.
" Buy me a new brazier ! " demanded Queenie.

2) " Once more over the top ! " ordered Commander.
" You first ! " conceded his troops.

3) The dissolution of the monasteries caused many disillusioned monks to pray secretly.

****

GAPS :

World War
II____

____

In Tudor
England______________________________________

____

Page 106

King
Edward____

>>______________________________________long
forgotten.

>>______________________________________Peace
Treaty.

>>__________________________________turned out.

>>_________________battle_____________________

____

>>____________________throne_________________

____

>>_________________empire_____________________

____

>>___ago_____________________________________

____

>>____chariots________________________________

>>__________royal palaces_________________ lost

CREATING BRAND NEW HISTORICAL LINE-STORIES

(Remembering :
** to draw on popular history and*
film interpretations of history:
the myth as well as the reality ;
** to avoid anything too clever*
or too detailed ;
** perhaps, to concentrate on*
some plans that never worked out.)

LINE-STORIES OF PHOTOGRAPHY

3 EXAMPLES :

1) All his masterpieces were black-and-white ;
his opinions too , predictably monochrome.

2) Her borrowed slides received so many prizes ;
her talented husband's, so few.

3) Witness our greatest living seaside photographer.
Witness his fleeing : " pervert, " " paedo, "
" predator."

****

GAPS :

Her newest
camera____

In the
Studio____
____

When
framed____

>>____not quite right.

>>____for the Exhibition.

>>____lost negatives.

________________________tripod_______________________

____

>>_______________________glorious sunshine__________

____

>>_______________________stage____________________

____

>>________Wedding_________________________________

____

>>_______Funeral__________________________________

>>_________riotous party__________________

____

CREATING BRAND NEW PHOTOGRAPHIC LINE- STORIES

(Remembering :
** to follow photography right through from intention to result ;*
** to imagine the pressures on some photographers to come up with the right image and right soon*
** and to think of what the persons being photographed actually think and feel.)*

LINE-STORIES IN THE CLASSROOM

3 EXAMPLES :

1) Told never to open his allocated desk, Ken did - and found drugs.

2) There was whispering all through Music - except when song lines needed whispering.

3) A horrible, malicious, note reached eleven pupils. The twelfth read it outloud.

****

GAPS :

Late one
Friday____

Feet
shuffled____

____

The teacher
tried____

________________________________with no success.

Page 112

>>_______________________________________ran out.

>>____________________________________nervous breakdown.

>>____________________their projects__________

____

>>_________________playtime___________________

____

>>_____________________visiting speaker_________

____

>>______books________________________________

____

>>______shouting______________________________

____

>>__________red herrings_____________________

____

CREATING BRAND NEW LINE STORIES SET IN A CLASSROOM

(*Remembering :*

* *your own schooldays :*
the fun and the tears ;
* *AND that the Classroom is a*
hotbed for incident ;
* *AND to emphase new*
visitors & Equipment
in the Classroom)

LINE STORIES SET IN PRISON

3 EXAMPLES :

1) " Lock him up ! " " Lose the keys ! "
Harangue, harass, hound...........he who hangs.

2) Wives seen through screens ; soaps viewed on screens ; drugs undiscovered by screens.

3) Wicked, intimidating, policeman : condemned, imprisoned. *Without* condemnation, imprisoned policeman wickedly intimidated.

****

GAPS :

Now locked
away____

Pentonville
boasted______________________________________

____

Page 115

The Prison
Chaplain____

>>____in the cells.

>>____no remorse.

>>____exercise yard.

>>_______________________chains__________________

____

>>______________________prison uniform___________

____

>>______________________remote island______________

____

>>_______warder__________________________________

____

>>_______super-grass______________________________

CREATING BRAND NEW LINE STORIES BASED ON PRISON

(*Remembering :*

* *Prison is a very artificial, restrictive, place ;*

* *Prisons tend to bring out the worst in almost everyone ;*

* *There is degradation, also falling apart within Prison walls.*)

LINE- STORIES IN A HOSPITAL

3 EXAMPLES :

1) The super-bug reached scared patients slower than
The Mail's super-bug scare story.

2) Nobody ever asked to see the leading surgeon's
Certificates : always " TO FOLLOW."

3) One << Professional Patient >> hijacked bed .
But screams, dying groans, hijacked his sleep.

GAPS :

In one
hospital____

___

Lights
out____

___

The
Matron____

____

>>____to

the morgue.

>>______________________________________yet
again.

>>_____________________________________after her
operation.

>>__________________theatre_____________________

____

>>____________________awkward customer__________

____

>>______________________NIL BY MOUTH________

____

>>______nurse__________________________________

>>__________two visitors_________________________

>>____________________ __long wait_______________

____

CREATING BRAND NEW LINE-STORIES AROUND HOSPITAL

(*remembering :*

** hospital wards are naturally interesting places ;*

** everyone in hospital is dependent on everyone else, staff included ;*

** medical drama can be borrowed from TV)*

LINE STORIES WITH AN AUTOBIOGRAPHICAL ANGLE

3 EXAMPLES :

1) Officially, my parents wrote this Autobiography.
I ghosted it.

2) Disarmingly, the Statesman's memoir : " told all. "
His dissenting daughter's memoir *told more.*

3) Devastatingly, a hero's papers were " all destroyed."
Heroically, certain (stolen) papers survived.

GAPS :

I remember________________________________

The PM's
Autobiography__________________________________

____

Page 121

This archive____

____

>>______________________________________to the last gasp.

>>___________________________diaries___________________

____

>>________________________news cuttings_______________

>>____________________eye-witnesses___________________

____

>>_________memory____________________________________

____

>>___________good impression_____________________

____

>>____________much effort____________________________

____

CREATING BRAND NEW AUTOBIOGRAPHICAL LINE - STORIES

(Remembering :
** to use imagination -*
as well as your own life story;
** to capture how <u>self-justifying</u> many autobiographies are*
** AND to cover well-lived and " blameless " lives)*

ADDITIONAL LINE-STORIES AROUND TRAVEL AND TRANSPORT

>> The 2005 Tube explosions closed the Underground to nervous Oliver. Forever.

>> " First-Class Train Accommodation is for First-Class Ticket-holders Only. " ONLY.

>> " Take away your fear of flying ! "
Of course. Off course. Hardly reassuring.

>> Listen to fellow passengers : attentively, unfailingly. Never face boredom again. Unless.....

>> Did the driver drive down the tunnel's dead- end deliberately ? Suicidally ? Altruistically ?

>> When fire engulfed the leading lorry,
no following lorry escaped the inferno.

>> One thousand train-spotters, one solitary juggernaut-spotter, out today.

>> Modern lorry-cab life is completely self-contained. He never got out.

>> They sail most who live furthest from the coast. Virtual reality !

<u>LINE-STORIES ANSWERING A QUESTION</u>

>> " How are you ? "
" Fine."
" And the weather ? "
" Fine."
" And the parking "
" Fine ! "

>> " Why name children ?"
" Simply tag them."
" Give them numbers."
" Keep them apart . "

>> " Must wash towels . "
" Don't ! "
" Why ever not ?"
" Towels dry clean bodies only ."

>> " Rhubarb ! "" Good rhubarb. "
" Sweet ? " " Not to-day's sweet."
" Good ! "

>> " DIY ? "
" See for yourself. "
" I did "
" Was it ? "
" It wasn't ! "
"….Worth seeing ?"

>> " Right ? " " No ! Left ! "
"Right ! "" No ! Left ! "
"That's right !" " Turn Left!"
" Too late. "

SUMMARY OF DOs AND DON'Ts :

Do make line-stories real stories ;

Do make line-stories interesting to read ;

Do make some line-stories have an unexpected ending ;

Do make line-stories progress from beginning to end ;

Do make line-stories out of varied subjects ;

Do make some line-stories suitably grim.

******

Don't make line-stories too clever ;

Don't make line-stories too complicated ;

Don't make line-stories unnecessarily vulgar ;

Don't make line-stories too trite and commonplace ;

Don't make line-stories bulge with long words ;

Don't make line-stories dependent on forced humour.

SPACE TO WRITE OVERSPILL LINE-STORIES :

HOW THE LINE-STORY MIGHT EVOLVE :

Perhaps overtaking the ubiquitous Su Doku ;

...........sitting alongside Crosswords in a newspaper ;

.... as a verbal challenge in speaking contests ;

.... as a decider in pub quizzes ;

.... as printing opposite the Greeting
in the middle of a Birthday Card ;

.... in common with certain poems, on the side
of a building, or in the Underground....

OR the line-story might stray into areas almost
unexplored in this particular book :

DOUBT, DISAGREEMENT, DEBT, DEATH, DREAD,
DISEASE, DISCOMFORT, DOMINANCE, DENIAL,
DISABILITY, DIVERSITY, DELIBERATION,
DISTRIBUTION, DESTITUTION,
CHANCE

[Was there ever a line-story,
was there ever a mini-saga, that did *not* speak of chance :
that did *not* depend on chance thoughts and words for
its successful completion ?]

About the Author :

Godfrey Holmes was born in Trowbridge, but spent his next 18 years in Bolton, Doncaster, Stoke-on-Trent and Withernsea (the unknown seaside resort of England ?).

Detailed study of Social Policy, Psychology and Criminology added the cities of Nottingham, Manchester and Liverpool to his list of interesting places.

He then had careers in teaching and in social work, whilst all the time writing for newspapers and magazines and finishing his books on *Truancy and Social Welfare*, also *Alcohol Among Young People.*

Starting in 2007, he has produced an impressive series of colour features on aspects of Derbyshire life and landscape, interspersed with speaking engagements throughout the North Midlands.

His pithy, sometimes witty, paragraphs frequently appear on Radio, TV or "*Letters to the Editor*" pages – and as winning entries to *New Statesman* competitions.

Godfrey's wider interests include Architecture, Coinage, Liturgy, the Coast of England & Wales, Railways and Rambling.

****

PRINTED BY:
Spire Graphics Ltd